POOH
THE BOUNCING BEAR

by Ronald Kidd
illustrated by Vaccaro Associates, Inc.

Grolier Books

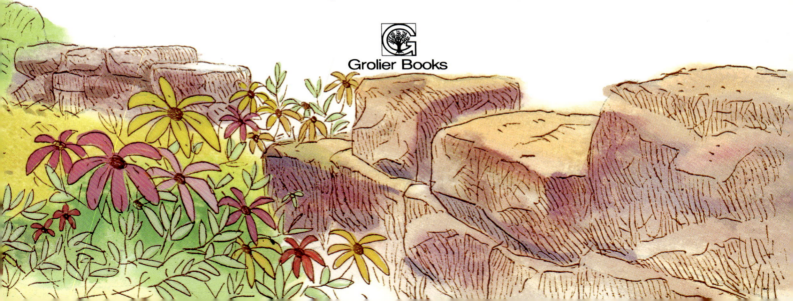

Based on the Pooh stories by A.A. Milne
[copyright the Pooh Properties Trust].

Edited by Ruth Lerner Perle
Produced by Graymont Enterprises, Inc.
Design and Art Direction by Michele Italiano-Perla
Pencil Layouts by Ennis McNulty
Painted by Lou Paleno

ISBN 0-7172-8446-8

Printed in the United States of America.

One summer morning, Winnie the Pooh was walking through the Hundred-Acre Wood with a close friend.

"Isn't it a nice day?" said Pooh. The friend didn't answer. Farther on, Pooh stopped to look at some daisies.

"Why do flowers grow up instead of down?" Pooh asked. The friend was silent.

After a while, Pooh said, "Don't you think it's time for a little something to eat?" The friend said nothing.

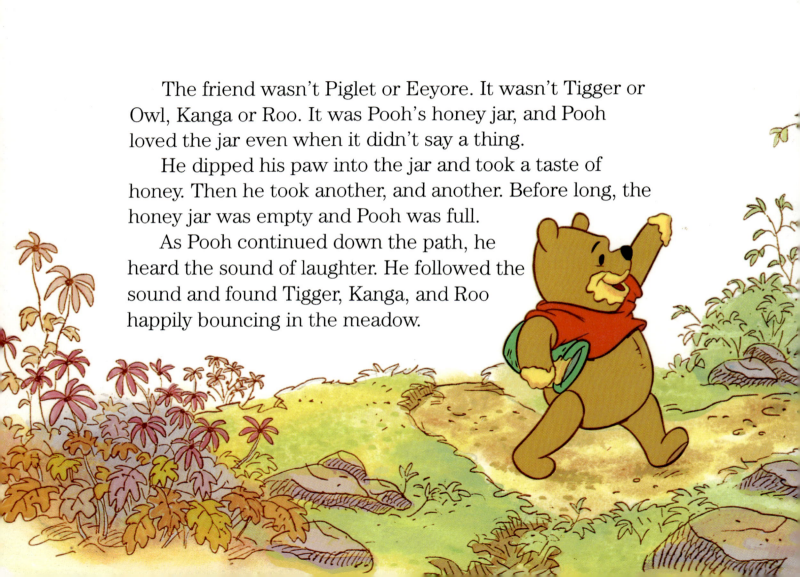

The friend wasn't Piglet or Eeyore. It wasn't Tigger or Owl, Kanga or Roo. It was Pooh's honey jar, and Pooh loved the jar even when it didn't say a thing.

He dipped his paw into the jar and took a taste of honey. Then he took another, and another. Before long, the honey jar was empty and Pooh was full.

As Pooh continued down the path, he heard the sound of laughter. He followed the sound and found Tigger, Kanga, and Roo happily bouncing in the meadow.

"Hello there, Pooh!" shouted Tigger. "It's a beautiful day for bouncin'!"

Roo called out, "Come on, Pooh. You try it!"

Pooh imagined himself flying past butterflies and birds, floating up over the clouds, laughing all the way. He could hardly wait to bounce.

3

Gripping the honey jar tightly, Pooh said, "Here I go!"
He bent his knees and sprang into the air.
It was a fine bounce, except that Pooh didn't leave the ground. What he did was fall over sideways.
Kanga helped him up, saying, "That jar looks heavy. Why don't you set it down and try again?"
"Yes, of course," said Pooh.

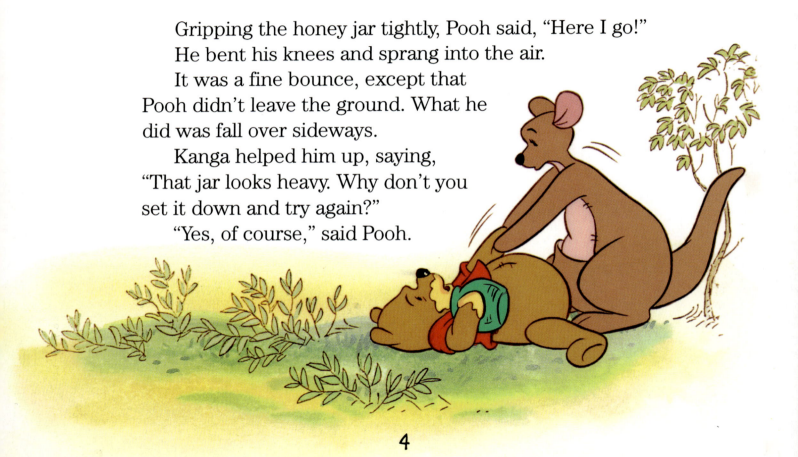

Pooh carefully placed his honey jar on the grass.
Then he closed his eyes and bounced as high as he could.
"How am I doing?" he asked, his eyes still closed.
"Could be bouncier," said Tigger.

Pooh opened his eyes. He hadn't moved.

"That's odd," said Pooh. "I thought I was making a bouncing sound."

"I don't think it was a bounce," said Roo. "It was more of a slosh."

Pooh tried again and again—standing still, on the run, off rocks, over logs. Nothing seemed to work.

"We're sorry, Pooh," said Kanga. "Maybe you should come back another time and try again."

6

Pooh picked up his honey jar and went home. That night, he dreamed of bouncing, and the dream turned into a song.

Who's that bouncing up and down
With a jar that's filled with honey?
He acts like Tigger but his fur is brown.
It's Winnie the Pooh! Isn't that funny?

Who's that floating past the trees,
Out of the forest and into the blue,
Light as a feather and round as you please?
It's Pooh the Bouncing Bear, that's who!

Pooh woke up the next morning, happy to be a
bouncing bear. He decided to celebrate by bouncing out of
bed. But once his dream had ended, so had his bounces.

Pooh wanted to bounce as high as he did in his dreams. But, being a bear of very little brain, he didn't know how. So he set out to ask his friends about it.

First he went to see Eeyore. He found the old gray donkey standing in a thistle patch.

"Good morning, Pooh," said Eeyore, "If it *is* a good morning. Which I doubt."

"Eeyore," Pooh said, "I can't bounce."

Eeyore shook his head sadly. "One more thing to worry about," he said.

"I thought perhaps I could learn," said Pooh.

"Of course you could," Eeyore said. "And while we're at it, I'll grow a second tail."

Pooh was pleased that Eeyore would have two tails.

"Do you think I could swing from them?" asked Pooh.

"No," said Eeyore. "You can't swing from them because it won't happen. I'm sorry to tell you this, Pooh, but donkeys don't have two tails. And bears don't bounce."

Discouraged, Pooh left the thistle patch. If bears didn't bounce, how could he ever be Pooh, the Bouncing Bear?

12

Next, Pooh went to see Owl, who was known as the wisest animal in the forest.

"Owl," said Pooh, "I was wondering—"

"You've come to the right place," Owl declared. "Wondering is a fine thing to do on a day such as this."

Pooh was pleased to hear it, even though he didn't know what a Daysuch was.

Pooh began again. "Eeyore was just telling me that bears don't bounce and donkeys don't have two tails."

"Tails?" said Owl. "Are you referring to my distant cousin, Tommy Tailspin?"

"Well, not exactly," said Pooh.

"Did I ever tell you how he got his name?"

"No," Pooh replied, "but—"

Owl continued, "It seems that Tommy wanted to be the fastest bird in the forest. Everyone told him that owls aren't built for speed, but Tommy wouldn't listen. Can you imagine that? He wouldn't listen!"

Pooh said, "Yes, I can imagine that."

"One day," Owl went on, "Tommy flew to the top of a tall tree. Then he dove toward the ground as fast as he could go. Halfway down, he started to spin. Luckily, there were some bushes under the tree. He never tried it again, but they still call him Tommy Tailspin. What do you think of that, Pooh? Pooh?"

Pooh was hurrying out the door. Hearing Owl talk about Tommy Tailspin gave Pooh an idea. The idea was a little like his dream, because in both of them, Pooh was bouncing.

Pooh went to see his friend Piglet and said, "Piglet, I need your help with an important idea."

"Oh, boy!" said Piglet.

"We'll need a balloon," Pooh said, "because it's a balloonish sort of idea."

Piglet found a balloon for Pooh, and together they walked through the forest until they found a tall oak tree.

18

"This tree should be just right," Pooh said.

"For what?" asked Piglet.

"For bouncing. Eeyore says that bears don't bounce. But perhaps they would if they started from a very high place, such as this tree."

"What's the balloon for?" Piglet said.

"You'll see."

With that, Pooh began to climb.

Halfway up the tree, Pooh heard a buzzing sound. He knew that where there is buzzing, there are bees. And where there are bees, there is honey.

"Pooh!" called Piglet from below. "Why did you stop climbing?"

"I thought I'd stop for a little snack," Pooh replied. "After all, bouncing is hard work."

21

When Pooh finished his
snack, he began climbing again.
In one way it was easier, because
his snack had given him energy.
But in another way it was harder,
because his paws tended to stick
to the tree.

22

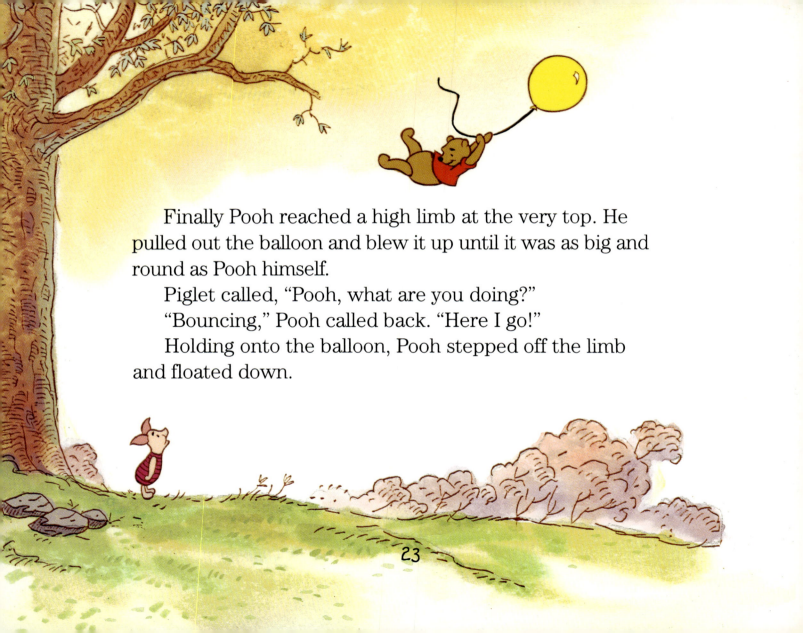

Finally Pooh reached a high limb at the very top. He pulled out the balloon and blew it up until it was as big and round as Pooh himself.

Piglet called, "Pooh, what are you doing?"

"Bouncing," Pooh called back. "Here I go!"

Holding onto the balloon, Pooh stepped off the limb and floated down.

He floated down, down, past the bees and over Piglet's head. When Pooh touched the ground, he bent his knees and tried to spring back up again. But his feet stayed firmly planted on the ground.

25

Piglet came running up, breathless. "How was it,
Pooh? How was your bounce?"

"Well," Pooh replied, "it wasn't a fast bounce. On the
other hand, it wasn't a slow bounce,
either. To tell the truth, Piglet, I
don't believe it was a bounce at all."

26

As Pooh shook his head sadly, he heard someone whistling. Christopher Robin came strolling down the path.

"Christopher Robin," said Pooh, "have you ever tried bouncing?"

"I've tried it," said Christopher Robin, "but I'm not very good at it."

"Some of us can't bounce at all," Pooh sighed.

27

"Pooh," said Christopher Robin gently, "bears aren't supposed to bounce."

"What are they supposed to do?" asked Pooh.

"They're supposed to eat honey and be kind to their friends."

"Isn't that lucky?" Pooh said. "Those are just the things I like to do."

Christopher Robin hugged Pooh and said, "Silly old bear."

Christopher Robin took Pooh's hand, and together with Piglet they walked to the meadow, where they found Tigger, Kanga, and Roo laughing and bouncing.

Pooh smiled and decided he could still be Pooh, the Bouncing Bear. He was bouncing inside, where bouncing really counts.

31